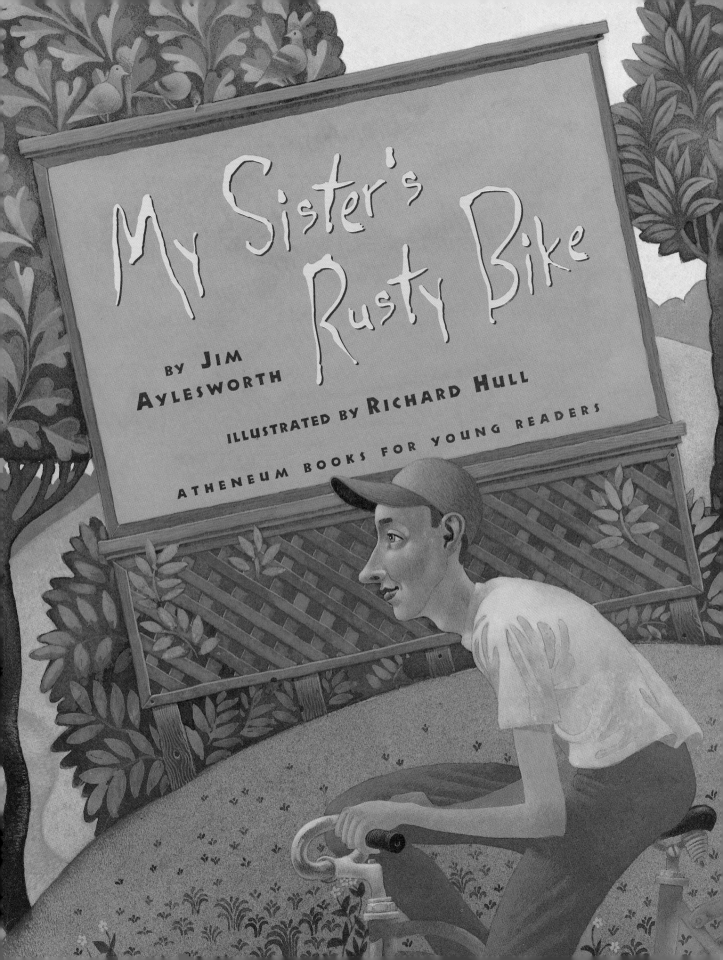

My Sister's Rusty Bike

BY JIM AYLESWORTH

ILLUSTRATED BY RICHARD HULL

ATHENEUM BOOKS FOR YOUNG READERS

I once rode round America
On my sister's rusty bike.
I found some crazy places and
Some folks I think you'll like.
I met some gals. I met some guys.
I met their critters too.
And though you may be dubious,
I swear that it's all true.

I rode to Massachusetts
On my sister's rusty bike,
And found just south of Marblehead
A place I think you'll like.
A gal lives there named Pat McDuff.
Her cats have purple fur.
They love to pile up in Pat's lap,
And as she pets, they purr.

I rode to Pennsylvania
On my sister's rusty bike,
And found just west of Stoney Run
A place I think you'll like.
A guy lives there named Gilly Gibbs.
His hens lay colored eggs.
In fact, they lay so many,
Gill gathers them in kegs.

I rode to West Virginia
On my sister's rusty bike,
And found just north of Paradise
A place I think you'll like.
A gal lives there named Dee Dee Lee.
She loves her pink pet sheep.
At night they sleep in bed with her
In one warm, woolly heap.

I rode to Indiana
On my sister's rusty bike,
And found just east of Farmersburg
A place I think you'll like.
A guy lives there named Buddy Biggs.
His cow has spots of blue.
I did not count her right side but
Her left has twenty-two.

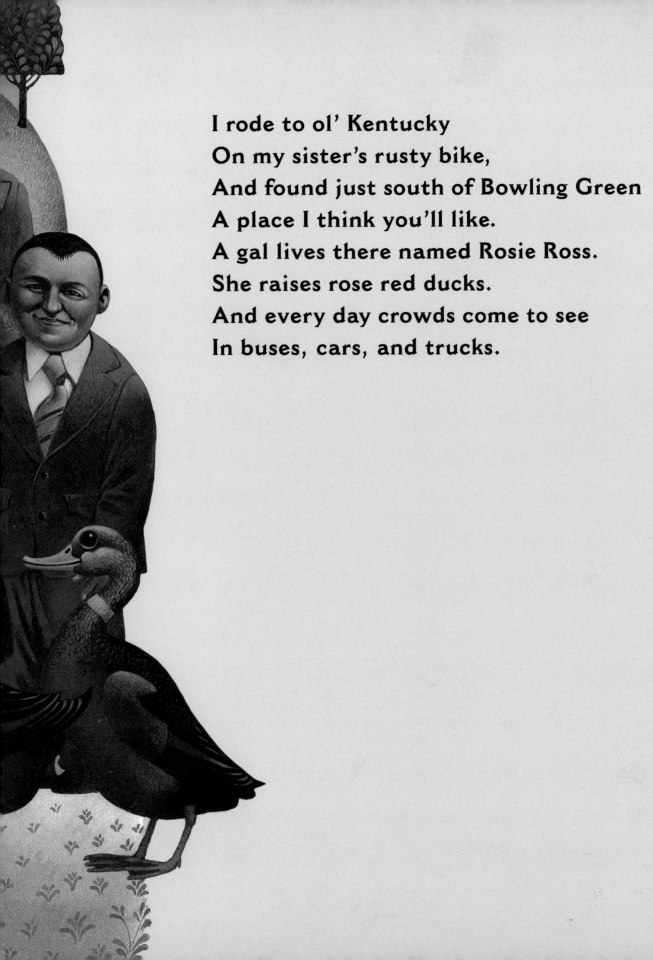

I rode to ol' Kentucky
On my sister's rusty bike,
And found just south of Bowling Green
A place I think you'll like.
A gal lives there named Rosie Ross.
She raises rose red ducks.
And every day crowds come to see
In buses, cars, and trucks.

I rode to Alabama
On my sister's rusty bike,
And found just west of Carbon Hill
A place I think you'll like.
A guy lives there named Willie Weems.
He's trained two dozen pigs.
And when Will gets his fiddle out,
They all start dancing jigs.

I rode to Mississippi
On my sister's rusty bike,
And found just north of Tupelo
A place I think you'll like.
A gal lives there named Maybelle Bean.
Her dog knows awesome tricks,
Like barking out the ABC's
And counting up to six.

I rode to Louisiana
On my sister's rusty bike,
And found just east of Shady Oaks
A place I think you'll like.
A guy lives there named Conroy Hicks.
His goats sing country tunes;
Sad songs about unlucky love,
And neon-lit saloons.

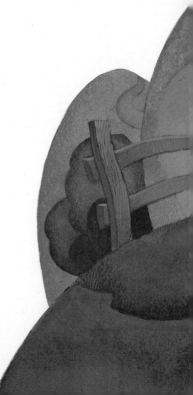

I rode to Oklahoma
On my sister's rusty bike,
And found just south of Cherokee
A place I think you'll like.
A gal lives there named Linda Dunn.
Her horse loves TV shows.
And when he wants the channel changed,
He does it with his nose.

I rode to Minnesota
On my sister's rusty bike,
And found just west of Granite Falls
A place I think you'll like.
A guy lives there named Jojo Jones.
His pets are pampered toads.
Old Jojo catches all their flies,
Then serves them à la mode.

I rode to Colorado
On my sister's rusty bike,
And found just east of Toonerville
A place I think you'll like.
A guy lives there named Benny Finn.
His rugs are living bears.
And when Ben plugs his vacuum in
They all jump on the chairs.

I rode to Arizona
On my sister's rusty bike,
And found just south of Iron Springs
A place I think you'll like.
A gal lives there named Dixie Nix.
She's very fond of snakes.
She treats them like her dearest friends
And feeds them pies and cakes.

I rode to California
On my sister's rusty bike,
And found just west of Santa Cruz
A place I think you'll like.
A guy lives there named Ike O'Day.
He owns a snow white crow.
He's taught it how to speak in rhyme
And quote from Edgar Poe.

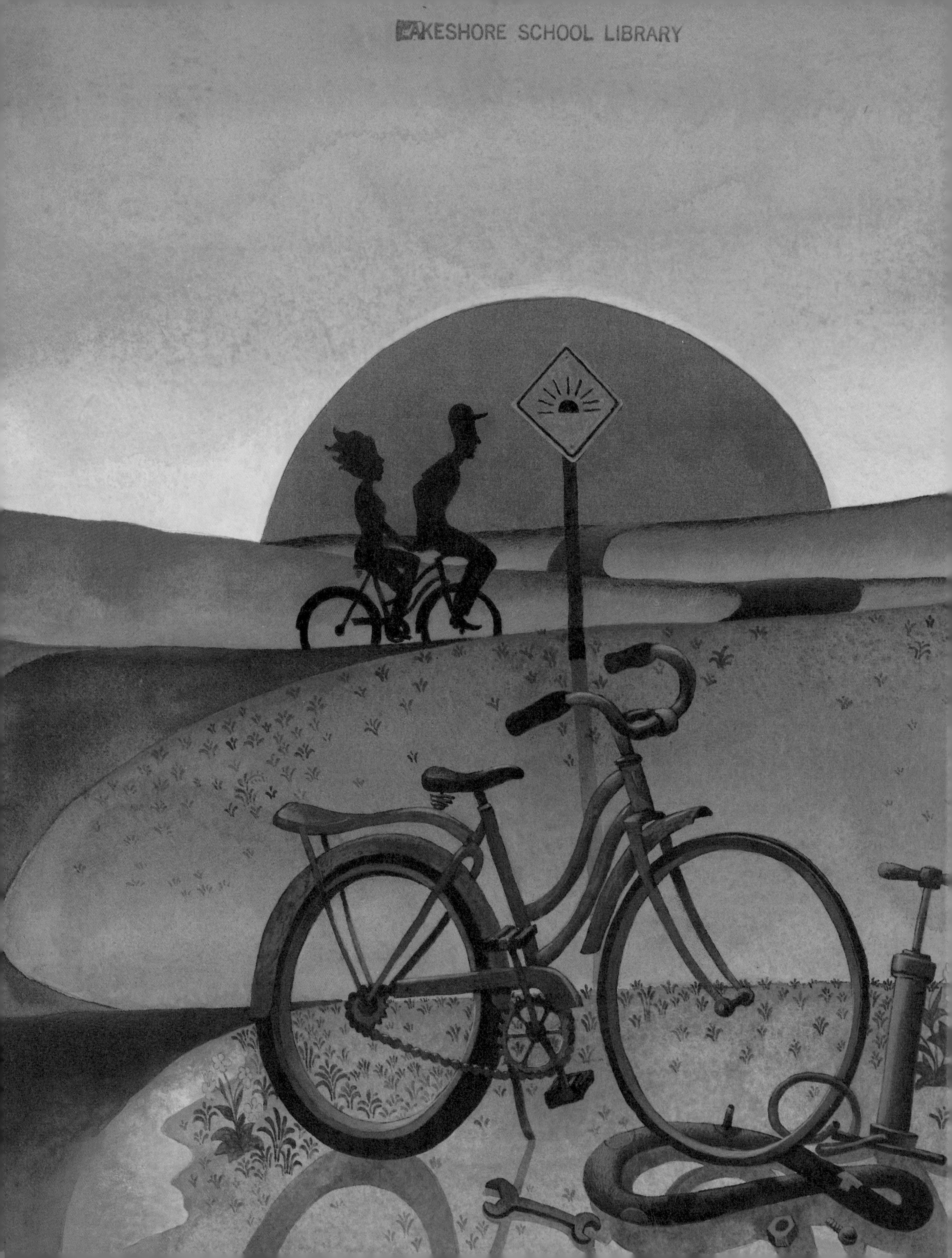

I want to keep on riding
On my sister's rusty bike,
But found out just this morning
My tire has hit a spike.
A gal I know, she just came by.
She'll take me into town,
And when I get a patching kit,
I'll be back riding round.

To the children of America, with love!
—J. A.

To Jonathan
—R. H.

Atheneum Books for Young Readers
An imprint of Simon & Schuster Children's Publishing Division
1230 Avenue of the Americas
New York, New York 10020

Text copyright © 1996 by Jim Aylesworth
Illustrations copyright © 1996 by Richard Hull

Book design by Becky Terhune
The text of this book is set in Cantoria.
The illustrations are rendered in gouache.

First edition
Printed in the United States of America

10 9 8 7 6 5 4 3 2 1

Library of Congress Cataloging-in-Publication Data
Aylesworth, Jim.
My sister's rusty bike / by Jim Aylesworth ; illustrated by Richard Hull. — 1st ed.
    p.   cm.
Summary: A rhyming tale of a zany, zigzag trip around America.
ISBN 0-689-31798-0
[1. Bicycles and bicycling—Fiction. 2. Travel—Fiction. 3. Tall tales. 4. Stories in rhyme.]
I. Hull, Richard, 1945– ill. II. Title
Pz8.3.A95Mw   1996
[E]—dc20   94-20117